ire

Catch!

For Kiona, Jermaine and Omari ~ T.C.
For Heather and Theo and happiness ~ K.W-M.

Scholastic Children's Books
Commonwealth House, 1-19 New Oxford Street
London WC1A 1NU, UK
a division of Scholastic Ltd
London ~ New York ~ Toronto ~ Sydney ~ Auckland
Mexico City ~ New Delhi ~ Hong Kong

First published in hardback in the UK by Scholastic Ltd, 2003
First published in paperback in the UK by Scholastic Ltd, 2003
This paperback edition first published in the UK by Scholastic Ltd, 2004

Text copyright © Trish Cooke, 2003
Illustrations copyright © Ken Wilson-Max, 2003

ISBN 0 439 98278 2

Printed in Singapore

2 4 6 8 10 9 7 5 3 1

The rights of Trish Cooke and Ken Wilson-Max
to be identified as the author and illustrator respectively
of this work have been asserted by them in accordance
with the Copyright, Designs and Patents Act, 1988.

Catch!

written by
Trish Cooke

illustrated by
Ken Wilson-Max

Hippo

It was a hot sunny afternoon.
Mum and Kiona were playing catch.

Mum threw a ball up in the air
and Kiona tried to catch it.

Catch!

But the ball
was too big and
Kiona could not get
her arms around it.
"Never mind," said Mum.
"Let's find something else."

Kiona looked.

She needed something
that was not as big as the ball.
She looked all around the garden
and then she saw it.
Kiona found . . .

. . . a berry.

Mum threw the berry up in the air
and Kiona tried to catch it.

Catch!

But the berry was too small
and Kiona did not see it coming down.

"Never mind," said Mum.
"We'll find something else."

Kiona looked and looked.

She needed something
that was not as big as the ball
and not as small as the berry.
Something in the middle.
She looked all around the garden
and then she saw it.
Kiona found . . .

. . . an apple.

Mum put Kiona up on her shoulders
and Kiona reached for the apple.

Catch!

But the apple was too hard and it hurt
Kiona's hand when it came down.
"Never mind," said Mum.
"Let's look for something else."

So they looked.
They needed something
that was not as big as the ball,
not as small as the berry
and not as hard as the apple.

Kiona looked everywhere
and then she saw it.
Kiona found . . .

. . . a balloon!

Mum threw the balloon up in the air
and Kiona tried to catch it.

Catch!

But the balloon was too soft
and it burst when Kiona touched it.

"Never mind," said Mum. "We'll find something else."

Mum and Kiona looked and they looked,
for something that was not as big as the ball,
not as small as the berry,
not as hard as the apple
and not as soft as the balloon.
They looked all around the house . . .

. . . but they couldn't find anything.
Kiona felt glum.

"I know," said Mum,
"let's have an ice cream."
And she put a big blob
on a cone for Kiona.
But when she gave it to her,
the ice cream was too
slippery . . .

. . . and it dropped and it dripped,
and it dripped and it dropped,

and it made a mess all over Kiona's dress.

"Bathtime!" said Mum.

Kiona put her sticky hands under the cold tap
and tried to catch the water.
But it splished and it splashed much too fast,
straight through her fingers.

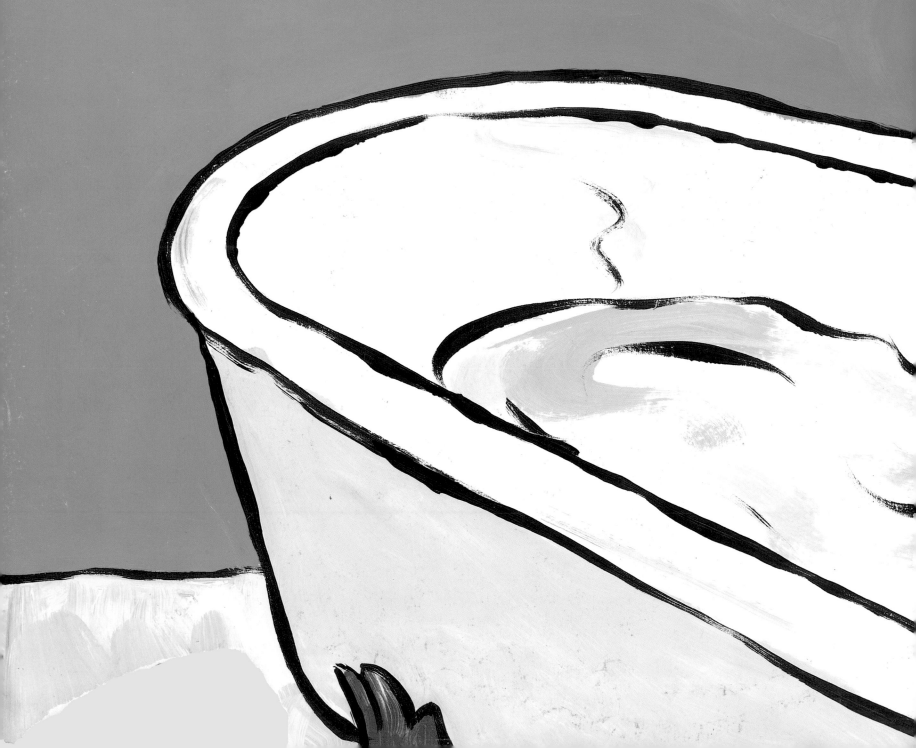

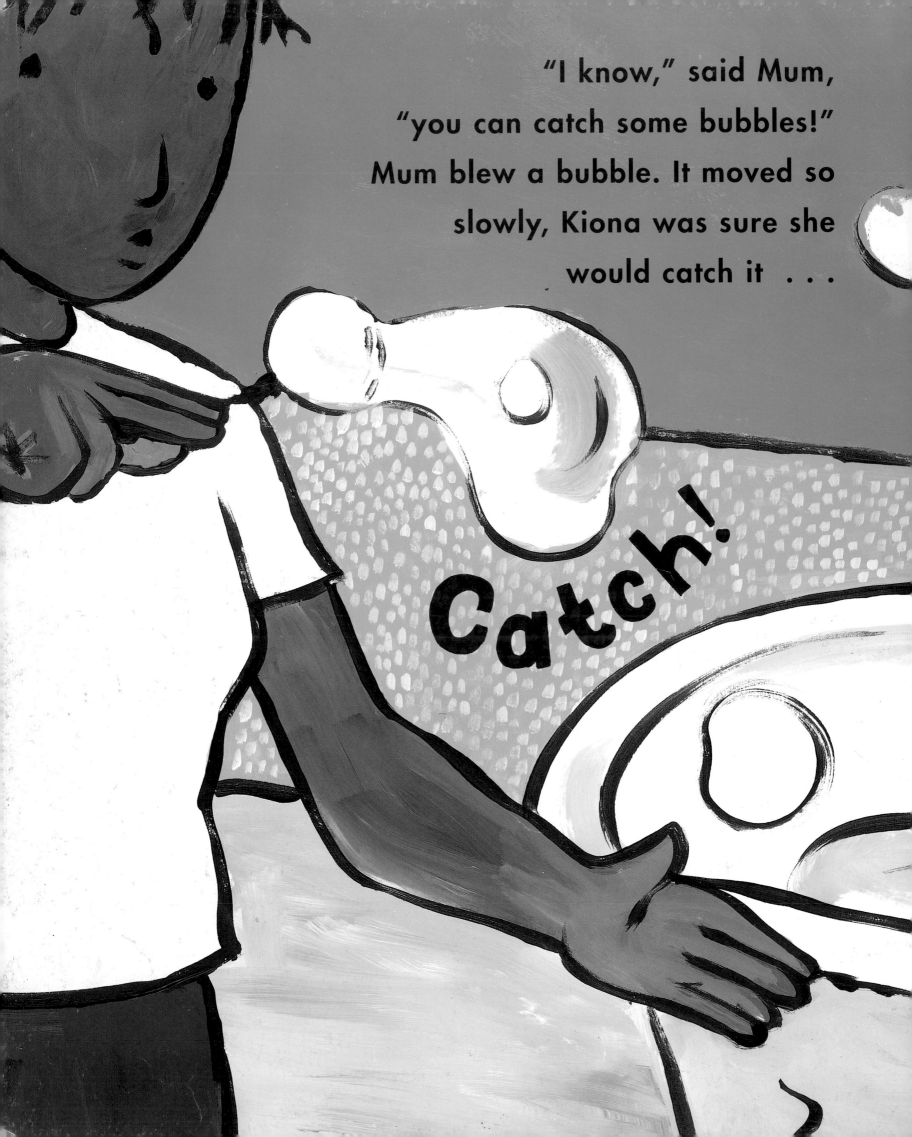

"I know," said Mum, "you can catch some bubbles!" Mum blew a bubble. It moved so slowly, Kiona was sure she would catch it . . .

Catch!

. . . but when she opened her hands, the bubble had gone!

"I can't catch anything," said Kiona.
Mum helped her get dry.
"There is something you can catch,"
said Mum. "Something very special.
It's not too big, it's not too small.
It's just about the right size."

Kiona wondered what it might be.

"It's not too hard,"
said Mum,
"it's not too soft.
It's not too slippery,
it's not too fast.
And it won't disappear
when you catch it.
When you catch this,
it stays with you
for ever and ever."

Mum helped Kiona
into bed.

"What is it? What is it?" Kiona gasped.
"Throw it to me now!"
Kiona stretched out her hands
and stood on her toes.

And when Mum blew her a kiss . . .

. . . Kiona caught it on her nose and it stayed there,
for ever and ever.